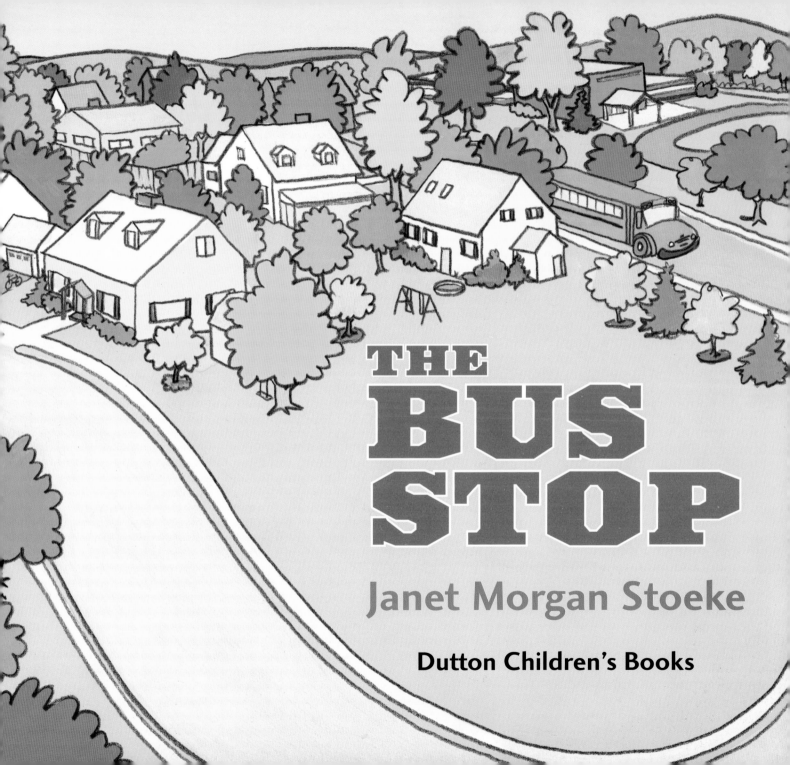

THE
BUS
STOP

Janet Morgan Stoeke

Dutton Children's Books

**Miranda Cook
has a library book.**

And she can't wait
to bring it
to the bus stop.

**Jackson Bowles
has a backpack that rolls.**

And he can't wait
to bring it
to the bus stop.

**Stevie Beecher
has a present for the teacher.**

**And he can't wait
to bring it
to the bus stop.**

Mrs. Simpson-Russ
got a brand-new bus.
And she can't wait to drive it
to the bus stop.

The bus looks
awfully big and tall.
Each kid feels
kind of scared and small.

But they can do it— they are brave!

Their parents see them
smile and wave.

School is great.
But they just can't wait . . .

to be riding back home
to the bus stop!

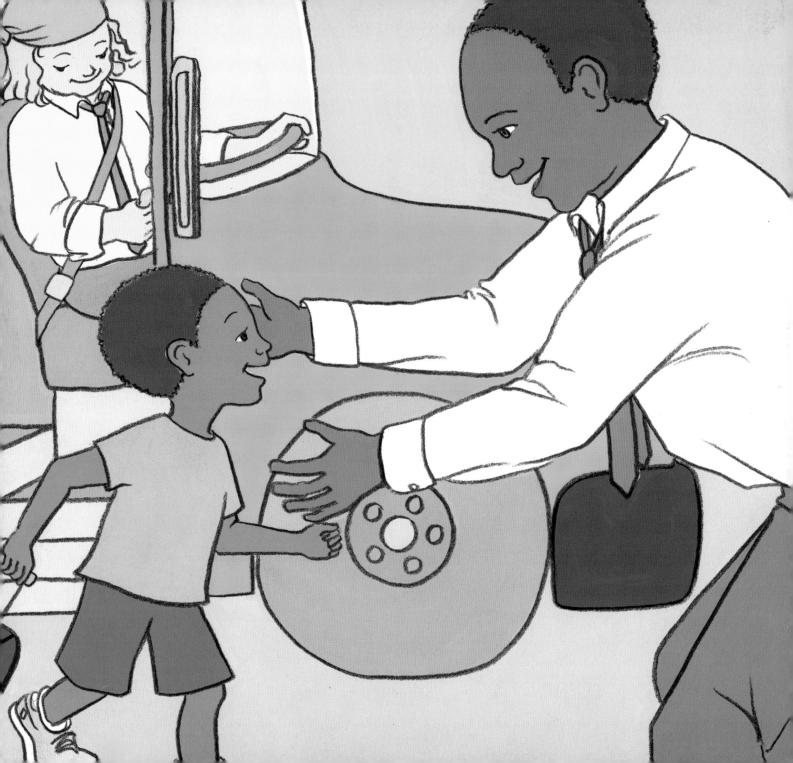

For Shirley Ann Kennedy

DUTTON CHILDREN'S BOOKS
A division of Penguin Young Readers Group

Published by the Penguin Group
Penguin Group (USA) Inc., 375 Hudson Street, New York, New York 10014, U.S.A. • Penguin Group (Canada
90 Eglinton Avenue East, Suite 700, Toronto, Ontario, Canada M4P 2Y3 (a division of Pearson Penguin Canada
Penguin Books Ltd, 80 Strand, London WC2R 0RL, England • Penguin Ireland, 25 St Stephen's Green, Dublin 2,
(a division of Penguin Books Ltd) • Penguin Group (Australia), 250 Camberwell Road, Camberwell, Victoria 3124,
(a division of Pearson Australia Group Pty Ltd) • Penguin Books India Pvt Ltd, 11 Community Centre, Panchshee
New Delhi - 110 017, India • Penguin Group (NZ), Cnr Airborne and Rosedale Roads, Albany, Auckland 1310, New
(a division of Pearson New Zealand Ltd) • Penguin Books (South Africa) (Pty) Ltd, 24 Sturdee Avenue, Roseb
Johannesburg 2196, South Africa • Penguin Books Ltd, Registered Offices: 80 Strand, London WC2R 0RL, Eng

Library of Congress Cataloging-in-Publication Data

Stoeke, Janet Morgan.
The bus stop / by Janet Morgan Stoeke.   p. cm.
Summary: Kindergartners gather for their exciting first ride on the school bus.
ISBN 978-0-525-47805-8 (hardcover)
[1. School buses—Fiction. 2. Stories in rhyme.] I. Title.
PZ8.3.S86835Bu   2007 [E]—dc22   2006024469

Published in the United States by Dutton Children's Books,
a division of Penguin Young Readers Group
345 Hudson Street, New York, New York 10014
www.penguin.com/youngreaders

Designed by Abby Kuperstock
Manufactured in China • First Edition
1 3 5 7 9 10 8 6 4 2